# LARGE PR

# NURSERY RHYMES

*Merry 1st Christmas Kale!*

*from Santa*

## Illustrated by David Crossley

**Brown Watson**
ENGLAND

# WEE WILLIE WINKIE

Wee Willie Winkie
Runs through the town,
Upstairs and downstairs
In his nightgown.

Rapping at the window,
Crying through the lock,
Are the children all in bed,
For it's past eight o'clock.

# HIGGELDY, PIGGELDY

Higgeldy, piggeldy, my black hen,
She lays eggs for gentlemen;
Sometimes nine and sometimes ten,
Higgeldy, piggeldy, my black hen.

# JACK AND JILL

Jack and Jill went up the hill,
To fetch a pail of water;
Jack fell down and broke his crown,
And Jill came tumbling after.

# BAA, BAA, BLACK SHEEP

Baa, baa, black sheep,
Have you any wool?
Yes, sir, yes, sir,
Three bags full.

One for the master,
And one for the dame,
And one for the little boy
Who lives down the lane.

# OLD MOTHER HUBBARD

Old Mother Hubbard
Went to the cupboard,
To get her poor doggy a bone;

But when she got there,
The cupboard was bare,
And so the poor doggy had none!

# TO BED, TO BED

"To bed, to bed!" said Sleepy Head.
"Tarry a while," said Slow.
"Put on the pan," said greedy Ann.
"We'll sup before we go."

# COCK-A-DOODLE DOO!

Cock-a-doodle doo!
My dame has lost her shoe,
My master's lost his fiddling stick,
And knows not what to do.

# LITTLE BOY BLUE

Little Boy Blue,
Come blow your horn,
The sheep's in the meadow,
The cow's in the corn.

Where is the boy
Who looks after the sheep?
He's under the haystack,
Fast asleep!

# HUMPTY DUMPTY

Humpty Dumpty sat on a wall,
Humpty Dumpty had a great fall.

All the King's horses
And all the King's men,
Couldn't put Humpty together again.

# ROCK-A-BYE BABY

Rock-a-bye baby,
On a tree top,
When the wind blows
The cradle will rock.

When the bough breaks,
The cradle will fall -
Down will come baby,
Cradle and all!

# THREE BLIND MICE

Three blind mice, three blind mice,
See how they run, see how they run!
They all ran after the farmer's wife,

Who cut off their tails
With the carving knife,
Did you ever see such a thing in your life,
As three blind mice?

# POLLY PUT THE KETTLE ON

Polly put the kettle on,
Polly put the kettle on,
Polly put the kettle on,
We'll all have tea.

Sukey take it off again,
Sukey take it off again,
Sukey take it off again,
They've all gone away.

# THE GRAND OLD DUKE OF YORK

Oh, the grand old Duke of York,
He had ten thousand men;

He marched them up to the top of the hill,
And he marched them down again.
And when they were up, they were up,
And when they were down, they were down,
And when they were only halfway up,
They were neither up nor down.

# LITTLE BO-PEEP

Little Bo-Peep has lost her sheep,
And doesn't know where to find them;

Leave them alone,
And they'll come home,
Wagging their tails behind them.

# LITTLE MISS MUFFET

Little Miss Muffet
Sat on a tuffet,
Eating her curds and whey;
There came a big spider,
Who sat down beside her,
And frightened Miss Muffet away.

# PAT-A-CAKE

Pat-a-cake, pat-a-cake, baker's man,
Bake me a cake as fast as you can;
Pat it and prick it and mark it with B,
And put it in the oven for baby and me.

# TO MARKET, TO MARKET

To market, to market,
To buy a fat pig,
Home again, home again,
Jiggety jig.

To market, to market,
To buy a fat hog,
Home again, home again,
Jiggety jog.

# TWO LITTLE DICKIE BIRDS

Two little dickie birds sittting on a wall,
One named Peter,
One named Paul.

Fly away, Peter!
Fly away, Paul!
Come back, Peter!
Come back, Paul!

# SING A SONG OF SIXPENCE

Sing a song of sixpence,
A pocket full of rye;
Four and twenty blackbirds
Baked in a pie.

When the pie was opened,
The birds began to sing;
Wasn't that a dainty dish
To set before the King.

The King was in his counting-house,
Counting out his money;
The Queen was in the parlour,
Eating bread and honey.

The maid was in the garden,
Hanging out the clothes,
When down came a blackbird
And pecked off her nose!

# SIMPLE SIMON

Simple Simon met a pieman
Going to the fair;
Said Simple Simon to the pieman:
"Let me taste your ware."

Said the pieman to Simple Simon:
"Show me first your penny."
Said Simple Simon to the pieman:
"Indeed, I have not any."

# HICKORY, DICKORY DOCK

Hickory, dickory dock,
The mouse ran up the clock.
The clock struck one,
The mouse ran down,
Hickory, dickory dock.

# DIDDLE, DIDDLE, DUMPLING

Diddle, diddle, dumpling, my son John,
Went to bed with his trousers on;
One shoe off and one shoe on,
Diddle, diddle, dumpling, my son John.

# OLD KING COLE

Old King Cole was a merry old soul,
And a merry old soul was he;

He called for his pipe,
And he called for his bowl,
And he called for his fiddlers three.

# THERE WAS A CROOKED MAN

There was a crooked man,
And he walked a crooked mile,
He found a crooked sixpence
Against a crooked stile;

He bought a crooked cat,
Which caught a crooked mouse,
And they all lived together
In a little crooked house.

# MARY HAD A LITLE LAMB

Mary had a little lamb,
Its fleece was white as snow,
And everywhere that Mary went
That lamb was sure to go.

It followed her to school one day,
That was against the rule;
It made the children laugh and play,
To see a lamb at school.

# THERE WAS AN OLD WOMAN

There was an old woman,
Who lived in a shoe,
She had so many children
She didn't know what to do;

She gave them some broth,
Without any bread,
She whipped them all soundly,
And sent them to bed.

# LADYBIRD, LADYBIRD

Ladybird, ladybird,
Fly away home.
Your house is on fire,
Your children are gone;

All except one,
And that's little Ann,
And she crept under
The warming pan.

# PUSSY CAT, PUSSY CAT

Pussy cat, pussy cat,
Where have you been?
I've been up to London,
To visit the Queen.

Pussy cat, pussy cat,
What did you there?
I frightened a little mouse,
Under a chair.

# HEY DIDDLE, DIDDLE

Hey diddle, diddle,
The cat and the fiddle,
The cow jumped over the moon.

The little dog laughed
To see such sport,
And the dish ran away with the spoon.

# JACK SPRAT

Jack Sprat could eat no fat,
His wife could eat no lean,
And so between them both,
They licked the platter clean.

Jack ate all the lean,
Joan ate all the fat,
The bone they picked it clean,
Then gave it to the cat.

# LITTLE POLLY FLINDERS

Little Polly Flinders
Sat among the cinders,
Warming her pretty little toes;

Her mother came and caught her,
And whipped her little daughter
For spoiling her nice new clothes.

# GOOSEY GANDER

Goosey, goosey gander,
Where shall I wander?
Upstairs and downstairs,
In my lady's chamber.

Where I met an old man,
Who wouldn't say his prayers,
I took him by the left leg,
And threw him down the stairs.

# DOCTOR FOSTER

Doctor Foster went to Gloucester
In a shower of rain;
He stepped in a puddle,
Right up to his middle,
And never went there again.

# IT'S RAINING,
# IT'S POURING

It's raining, it's pouring,
The old man is snoring.
He went to bed
And bumped his head,
And couldn't get up in the morning!

# RUB-A-DUB-DUB

Rub-a-dub-dub,
Three men in a tub,
And who do you think they be?

The butcher, the baker,
The candlestick-maker,
And up they jump all three!

# THIS LITTLE PIGGY

This little piggy went to market,
This little piggy stayed at home,
This little piggy had roast beef,
This little piggy had none.
And this little piggy cried,
"Wee, wee, wee," all the way home!

# JACK BE NIMBLE

Jack be nimble,
Jack be quick,
Jack jump over
The candlestick.

# I HAD A LITTLE NUT TREE

I had a little nut tree,
Nothing would it bear
But a silver nutmeg
And a golden pear.

The King of Spain's daughter
Came to visit me,
And all for the sake
Of my little nut tree.

# SEE-SAW MARGERY DAW

See-saw Margery Daw,
Johnny shall have a new master;
He shall have but a penny a day,
Because he can't work any faster.

# LITTLE TOMMY TITTLEMOUSE

Little Tommy Tittlemouse
Lived in a little house;
He caught fishes
In other men's ditches.

# TWEEDLEDUM AND TWEEDLEDEE

Tweedledum and Tweedledee
Agreed to fight a battle,
For Tweedledum said Tweedledee
Had spoiled his nice new rattle.

Just then flew by a monstrous crow,
As black as a tar barrel,
Which frightened both the heroes so,
They quite forgot their battle.

# HALF A POUND OF TUPPENNY RICE

Half a pound of tuppenny rice,
Half a pound of treacle,
That's the way the money goes,
Pop goes the weasel!

Up and down the city road,
In and out the Eagle,
That's the way the money goes,
Pop goes the weasel!

# I HAD A LITTLE PONY

I had a little pony,
His name was Dapple Gray;
I lent him to a lady,
To ride a mile away.

She whipped him,
She slashed him,
She rode him through the mire;
I would not lend my pony now,
For all the lady's hire.

# INDEX